THE SQUIRREL, THE HARE AND THE LITTLE GREY RABBIT

By Alison Uttley
Pictures by Margaret Tempest

templar publishing

A LONG TIME AGO, in a little house on the edge of a wood, there lived a hare, a squirrel and a little grey rabbit.

The hare, who wore a blue coat on weekdays and a red coat on Sundays, was a conceited fellow.

The squirrel, who wore a brown dress on weekdays and a yellow dress on Sundays, was proud.

But the little rabbit, who always wore a dress with a white collar and cuffs, was not proud at all.

Every morning, when the birds began to twitter, she sprang out of her bed in the attic and ran downstairs to the kitchen. She went into the shed for firewood, and lit the fire. Then she filled her kettle with clear water from the brook that ran past the door, just beyond the garden.

While the water boiled she swept the floor and dusted the kitchen. She made tea from daisy-heads in a brown teapot. Then she laid the table, put a bunch of lettuce leaves on each plate, and called Squirrel and Hare.

"Squirrel, Hare, wake up – breakfast is ready!"

Downstairs they strolled, rubbing their eyes and wriggling their ears.

"Good morning, Grey Rabbit," yawned Hare. "I declare you have given us lettuce again. Really, my dear, you must think of something new for breakfast."

"Good morning, Grey Rabbit," said Squirrel. "Where's the milk?"

"It hasn't come yet," she said.

"Tut," exclaimed Squirrel. "Late again."

Just then there was a tapping at the door. Little Grey Rabbit ran to open it, and there stood Hedgehog with a pint of milk.

"I nearly didn't get here at all," he said. "A dreadful thing has happened! A weasel has come to live in the wood. It isn't safe to be out after dusk."

"Oh dear!" replied Grey Rabbit. "You must take care you don't get caught, even if we *do* go without milk."

"Bless your heart," smiled Hedgehog. "You shall have milk as long as old Hedgehog has some prickles left. Well, good day, and warn those two grumblers in there."

"Whatever have you been talking about all this time?" asked Squirrel angrily.

Little Grey Rabbit drew her chair close. "Hedgehog says a weasel has come to live in the wood."

"A weasel?" said Squirrel. "Pooh! Who's afraid of a weasel?"

But she shut the window and poked the fire, and kept the poker in her hand while she drank her milk.

A *tap, tap, tap* came on the door.
"Who's that?" asked Squirrel.

Grey Rabbit opened the door a crack. "It's only Robin Redbreast with the letters," cried she. "Come in Robin, you quite startled us. Have you heard the news?"

"About the weasel? Yes. He's a great big fellow with very sharp teeth. Well, I must be off, I have to warn the birds," he said, and away he flew.

"Oh dear," said Grey Rabbit. "Perhaps I'd better not go out today."

"But I need a new teasel brush," cried Squirrel. "My tail is quite tangled."

"And I want some carrots," said Hare. "I'm tired of lettuce for breakfast."

So Little Grey Rabbit set off, with her basket on her arm. She kept a sharp lookout in the wood, and ran so softly that the leaves underfoot scarcely moved.

She found some teasel bushes growing in the hedge. She bit off three prickly heads and put them in her basket.

Then she ran on till she got to the
farmer's garden. One by one, she
carefully pulled up some carrots and
placed them in her basket.

"I wish we could grow carrots at
home," she said.

Suddenly, she heard an angry shout.
A sack was thrown over her head and
someone hit wildly at her with a rake.

Little Grey Rabbit ran this way and
that as she tried to dodge the blows.
Then she darted out through a hole in
the sack. She ducked in and out of the
cabbage leaves, with the farmer running
after, close to her heels.

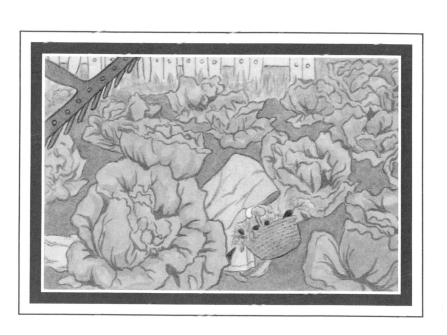

"You little rascal!" called the farmer. "You've been after my carrots. Just wait till I catch you."

But Little Grey Rabbit did not wait. She could not stop to explain that she thought they were everybody's carrots. She ran for her life, across the field to the wood.

"I don't think I shall go there again," she said, as she put a dock-leaf bandage on her hurt paw. "We must grow our own carrots. I will ask Wise Owl how to do it."

She hurried through the wood, and reached home safely.

"What a long time you have been," grumbled Hare. "Did you get my carrots?"

Little Grey Rabbit cooked dinner and gathered firewood. She was never still for a moment, but Hare and Squirrel sat beside the fire and never moved except to put fresh wood on the blaze.

When Hare and Squirrel had gone to bed, Little Grey Rabbit slipped outside. The moon was big and the stars winked and smiled at her. Everywhere was silver white, and Little Grey Rabbit could not help turning head over heels for joy.

She jumped the brook three times, then trotted into the wood. She noticed her feet left a trail of footprints in the grass, so she turned round and walked backwards.

At last she reached Wise Owl's house, a hollow oak tree. He sat on a bough, his shining eyes searching the wood.

Little Grey Rabbit waved a white handkerchief for a truce, and he nodded down at her.

"Wise Owl," she began, "will you tell me how to grow carrots?"

"What will you give me in return?" hooted Wise Owl.

"Oh dear, I haven't anything," she said sadly.

"Yes, you have," cried Owl. "You can give me your tail."

"My tail?" she exclaimed in horror.

"Yes, your tail," said Wise Owl, "or I shall not help you."

"You can have it," Little Grey Rabbit cried bravely. "But be quick."

So Wise Owl hopped down and, with one bite of his strong beak, he cut it off. Then he fastened it on his front door as a door knocker.

"You can grow carrots with carrot seed," he said.

"Where can I get it?" asked Little Grey Rabbit.

"From the shop in the village." Then he flapped his wings and flew away.

Little Grey Rabbit started for home. Now and then a shiny round tear fell on the grass, and she gave a sigh.

Suddenly, she turned a corner and saw the weasel! His back was turned; he was examining her footprints.

"Ah!" he cried. "A rabbit has gone this way!"

The weasel followed the footprints towards the brook, but when he reached it he was puzzled, for the footprints ran towards the water's edge on both sides. He scratched his whiskers.

"She must have tumbled in and been drowned," he said, and went off down the stream.

Little Grey Rabbit ran home and slept till the birds began to sing.

In the morning Hare stared at her. "Whatever have you done with your tail?" he asked.

"I gave it to Wise Owl," said Grey Rabbit, hanging her head.

"Disgraceful," said Hare.

"Disgracefuller," said Squirrel, not to be outdone.

A big tear ran down into Grey Rabbit's tea. She wished Wise Owl would give her back her tail.

After dinner she set off for the village, leaving Squirrel and Hare dozing by the fire. They did not see her go, nor did they see a black nose appear at the window.

When Little Grey Rabbit got to the village it was very quiet. No one saw her hesitate a moment outside the shop, then run through the open door.

She gazed about her with wide-open eyes. Wonderful things lay all about: buckets and frying pans, pots and cheeses, mouse-traps and cherry brandy. But would she ever find the seeds? Then she saw a picture of a carrot on a little packet, lying with other packets. Success at last! Here were lettuces and radishes, parsley and cabbages.

She seized one of each. Then she saw a bag with a yellow bird on it labelled 'Canary Seed', so she took that too.

As she ran home, she made her plans. "I shall sow three rows of carrot seeds, and the radishes next to them, and the parsley next. Then I'll sow the bird seed and have some little yellow birds as well."

She ran down the street and saw no one, except for five ducks waddling across the road.

"Ah," she went on, "I may get hundreds and hundreds of little birds from this bag... Goodness me, what's this?" For she had reached home and the front door stood wide open. No one was there.

In the kitchen the chairs were upset and the table pushed on one side. Bits of red hair from Squirrel's tail lay on the floor.

"Oh my dear Squirrel, my darling Hare," she cried, tears running down her cheeks. "Has that bad weasel got you?"

She took a pair of scissors, a rope and a stick, and started out to look for her companions.

On the other side of the brook the grass was flattened, as if a heavy object had been pulled along.

"He has put them in a bag and dragged them home," she murmured. "Poor, poor things!"

She hurried along the path, which took her through dark and gloomy glades. At last she came to an ugly black house with thick smoke coming out of the chimney.

She lay down under a bush and waited.

Soon the door opened and the savage weasel stood in the doorway.

"I shall need more sticks for the fire after all," he said. "They will be safe in there."

He shut the door and turned the key in the lock, then ran among the bushes, picking up sticks.

"Too-whit, too-whoo," called Wise Owl, as he flew overhead. The weasel looked up. He was afraid of Wise Owl, and he dared not move.

Grey Rabbit made a dash, turned the key, and was in the house while the weasel still gazed up at the owl overhead.

Little Grey Rabbit called, "Hare, Squirrel, where are you? It's me, it's Rabbit."

"Here, here! Oh save us, dear Grey Rabbit," cried two piteous voices from a bag under the sofa.

Quickly Rabbit cut the bag open and let the two unhappy ones out, but they were so bruised and weak they could hardly walk.

"Upstairs with you," cried Grey Rabbit, as she heard the weasel returning. "Take this rope and let yourselves out of the window. I will follow."

Then she seized a stool and crept into the bag, just as the weasel came in.

Grey Rabbit squeaked and moaned, and the weasel chuckled as he piled wood on the fire.

Upstairs Squirrel and Hare fastened the rope to a bedpost and slid down into the nettles. Away they went, struggling over brambles and across ditches.

The weasel opened the oven door, putting some dripping in the roasting tin. "I'll cook them both together," he said.

He took a stick and came over to the bag. Then he raised the stick and — *bang!* — down it came. Grey Rabbit crept inside the stool and lay protected by its legs. She didn't make a sound.

"Dead, both dead," said the weasel.

As he took hold of the hot roasting tin, Grey Rabbit slipped out of the bag, gave him a great push into the tin, and shut the oven door.

Off she ran, never stopping till she got home. As she sat panting in an armchair, the other two limped in.

"Oh, Grey Rabbit," they said, "we are very sorry. We shall never be proud or rude again. You saved us from the weasel, and if he ever comes back—"

"He won't, he is roasted by now," she interrupted, and told them all her adventures.

So they all lived happily together, and had a fine crop of radishes, carrots and onions, but no little yellow birds ever came up.

And sometime, I will tell you how Grey Rabbit got her tail back again…

A TEMPLAR BOOK

This edition first published in the UK in 2012 by Templar Publishing,
an imprint of The Templar Company Limited,
The Granary, North Street, Dorking, Surrey, RH4 1DN, UK
www.templarco.co.uk

Original edition first published in the UK in 1929 by William Heinemann

This edition edited by *Susan Dickinson* and *Emily Hawkins*
Additional design by *janie louise hunt*

1 3 5 7 9 10 8 6 4 2

ISBN 978-1-84877-263-2

Printed in China